STORIES FROM
✡ ✡ ✡ *the* ✡ ✡ ✡
JEWISH
WORLD

Written by Sybil Sheridan

Illustrated by Olivia Rayner

MACDONALD YOUNG BOOKS

First published in Great Britain in 1998
by Macdonald Young Books,
an imprint of Wayland Publishers Ltd

Macdonald Young Books
61 Western Road
Hove
East Sussex
BN3 1JD

Find Macdonald Young Books on the
internet at: http://www.myb.co.uk

Text © Sybil Sheridan 1987

Illustration © Olivia Rayner 1998

Editor: Rosie Nixon
Designer: Dalia Hartman

© Macdonald Young Books 1998

A CIP catalogue record for this book is
available from the British Library

ISBN 0 7500 2556 5

Printed and bound in Portugal by

Edições ASA

CONTENTS

THE LIE AND EVIL ENTER THE ARK

*Long ago the earth was corrupt and full of violence,
and God arranged a flood to wipe out all the wickedness in the
world. God told Noah to build an ark for his family and for two
of every living creature.*

One day, the Lie came to Noah and said, 'It will rain soon, please may I have a ride in your ark?'

'No,' said Noah, for he did not like the look of the Lie.

'Why not? You have so much space and you are welcoming all the other creatures,' said the Lie.

Noah did not know what to say – he had asked every type of animal to join him in the ark so he would need a good excuse to refuse the Lie. Then he thought of one.

'I am only taking pairs,' he said. 'If you can find a partner, you too can come on board.'

The Lie went off to find a partner, but every animal he asked ran away. Nobody liked him. The days went by, and the skies got darker. The Lie knew he would have to find someone soon or the ark would leave without him.

He looked here and there and everywhere. At last he found a likely person. Her name was Evil, and she was as unpleasant as he was himself. The Lie went up to her and explained his problem.

'Will you marry me?' he asked. Evil had never had a proposal before.

'Yes,' she said.

Hand in hand they ran as fast as they could to the ark.
Rain began to fall and Noah was pulling up the gangplank as
they arrived.

'Wait for us,' the Lie shouted, 'I have found a partner. You
cannot refuse me now.' Sadly, Noah let the Lie and Evil into
the ark.

For forty days and forty nights it rained and the whole earth was flooded. For forty days and forty nights the Lie and Evil made themselves comfortable amongst the pairs of animals. Then the rain stopped and dry land appeared. Noah let down the gangplank and the animals went out two by two.

As they left the ark, God blessed them all, saying:
'Be fruitful and multiply and replenish the earth.'
Everyone did so. The animals had offspring and Noah and his sons had several children. The Lie and the Evil produced many little lies and evils which grew and multiplied until the earth was once again full of the wickedness that God had sought to destroy.

HOW JUDAH SAVED THE JEWS

*A long time ago, there lived a mighty ruler called Antiochus.
His empire stretched over many lands, and everywhere the people
obeyed his command to worship the Greek god Zeus. In every land,
that is, except Israel.*

The Jews kept their own faith – they worshipped only God
and refused to bow down to Zeus. Antiochus did not like that.
He decided to teach the Jews a lesson. He sent his army to
attack the Temple in Jerusalem. They took away all the gold
and silver ornaments, they snuffed out the Eternal Lamp that
was always kept burning as a symbol of God's presence, and
they set up a statue of Zeus on the altar. Then, Antiochus
issued a decree. Every Jew must offer a pig as a sacrifice to
Zeus – or die.

In the village of Modin, an old priest named Mattathias went with his five sons to the market square to hear a soldier read out the decree. In the centre of the square was a huge statue.

'Who will be the first to worship Zeus?' the soldier asked.

There was much muttering and mumbling. Nobody wanted to sacrifice, but nobody wanted to die either.

Finally one man came forward and bowed down to the statue. Up leaped Mattathias! He grabbed a sword and killed the man.

'What the...?' the soldier began. But he could say no more – Mattathias had killed him too.

'Whoever is for God,' he shouted, 'follow me!'

Mattathias, with his sons and many of the villagers, ran into the hills to hide. Word spread quickly, and soon others joined them; all of them ready to defy Antiochus and worship God. They hid in the mountains by day. At night, they crept out to ambush army patrols and to tear down the statues of Zeus.

Antiochus soon heard of this and sent all the forces he had in Israel to wipe them out. The Jews organized themselves into a small army. Mattathias's son, Judah, took command.

'How can we possibly win?' people asked him.

'There are so few of us and Antiochus's army is huge.'

'Size is of no importance,' replied Judah. 'We are fighting for our lives and for our God. Our strength will come from him.'

Although his men were few in number, they had great faith and great courage. Every time they fought their enemy, they won.

In time, Antiochus mustered all the troops he had in his empire. An army of thousands marched into Israel and set up camp. Their plan was this. At night, while most of the army stayed in the camp to appear as if nothing was happening, a small battalion would seek out the Jews' stronghold and massacre them all.

Judah heard of the plan and as the battalion neared their hideout, the Jews stole softly away. The enemy found the place deserted. But at the very same time, the Jews entered the main camp and killed the soldiers there. The battalion returned to find, not their own men, but a heap of dead bodies – and Judah and his army.

'Run!' shouted their leader, and they ran.

Once the last of the enemy had left the country, Judah went to Jerusalem and entered the Temple. What a mess it was in! Curtains were torn, and ornaments broken. There were animals wandering around the rooms. Judah and his men would have to clean it up, but where should they begin?

'The first thing to be done,' said Judah, 'is to light the Eternal Lamp.'

He soon found it, but could find no oil with which to light it. All the jars of oil had been overturned, leaving a sticky mess on the floor. He searched and searched without any success.

Then, in a corner, he saw a tiny jug. It had a little oil in it – enough to keep the lamp burning for a day. What was Judah to do? Fresh oil supplies were four days' journey away. He could wait till more oil was brought, or light the lamp now and hope for the best.

'We should celebrate God's triumph now,' he said, and lit the lamp.

Then a strange thing happened. The amount of oil in the lamp was tiny – but it kept on burning. It burned for eight days – long enough for the new supplies to arrive.

Some say this was a miracle. Others say a greater miracle was the fact that Judah and his small group of followers could conquer the huge army of Antiochus. As the Bible itself tells us:

' "Not by might, but by My Spirit," says the Lord.'

THE OVERCROWDED HOUSE

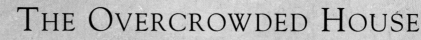

*There are many stories about poor people who grow rich,
but in real life most poor people remain so all their lives.
Here is a story about one of them.*

There once lived a poor Jew, in a tiny hovel on
the edge of a small village. He had a wife, seven
children, a cow, a goat and five chickens. Life was
not too bad for the family: the cow and the goat
gave them enough milk and cheese, and the
chickens provided eggs. They did not starve.
But, the man had one big worry – his house
was too small. He went to his Rabbi.

'Rabbi, Rabbi,' he said. 'What am I to do?
We are nine people living in one room – there is
hardly any space in which to turn around.'

16

The Rabbi thought for a moment. 'You have a cow?' he asked.

'Yes, I have a cow,' the man replied.

'Then take your cow into the house with you.'

The man did as the Rabbi told him. But the next week, he went again to the Rabbi.

'Rabbi, Rabbi,' he said, 'it is even worse than before! The cow takes up so much space, there is barely any room to breathe.'

The Rabbi sat and thought. 'You have a goat?' he asked.

'Yes, I have a goat,' replied the man.

'Then take your goat into the house as well.'

The next day the man saw the Rabbi again.

'Rabbi, Rabbi,' he said, 'it is even worse now that the goat is in the house, she smells so.'

'You have chickens?'

'Yes,' said the man, 'I have chickens.'

'Well then' said the Rabbi. 'Take the chickens into the house also.'

The next week the man knocked once more on the Rabbi's door.

'Rabbi, Rabbi, I cannot stand this any longer! Five chickens flying about the house – the feathers get everywhere – and the noise! You should hear it! It is unbearable. What am I to do?'

The Rabbi sat and thought.

'You should take the cow, the goat and the chickens out of your house and put them back where they were before.'

The next week, the man did not go to see the Rabbi, but the Rabbi saw him, praying happily in the synagogue.

'Well?' the Rabbi asked. 'How is it now at home?'

'Oh Rabbi,' said the man, 'it is wonderful! Now that I have taken out the cow, the goat and the chickens, there is so much room!'

HANNAH SENESH

In September 1939, eighteen year old Hannah Senesh left her home in Hungary and boarded a boat for Palestine. Hannah was sad to leave her family and her friends, but she knew that, in Hungary, she could never go to university or get a good job, because she was a Jew and at that time, life was very hard for the Jews.

The Second World War had just started. Hitler's German army was marching through Europe and Hungary was his ally. The Germans rounded up all the Jews, and put them in prisons or concentration camps. Hannah Senesh, like many young Jews, went to Palestine – the land called Israel in the Bible. They hoped to build a new Israel there, where Jews could live freely and not be persecuted.

In Palestine, Hannah learned to be a farmer. She spent her days picking oranges and milking cows, but she heard much about the war in Europe. Her mother wrote to her and told her how her brother George had escaped to Paris and hoped to join Hannah soon. Hannah asked her mother to come too, but she replied she could not leave.

'I am happy though, that my children are safe,' she said.

At that time, Palestine was ruled by Britain. Some of the Jews there joined the British army to fight against the Germans and Hannah volunteered for the Air Force.

In March 1944 she set off with six others on a daring mission. They were dropped by parachute into Yugoslavia, where they rescued British soldiers held prisoner by the Germans. Then, they moved on, crossing the border into Hungary. Their aim was to help the Jews escape from the clutches of the Nazis. But soon, Hannah was caught by German soldiers and sent to prison.

Soldiers beat her and tortured her, but she would not tell them what her mission was.

One day, the commandant sent for her.

'We have a surprise for you,' he said. Hannah was pushed
into the next room and there she saw her mother!

'Hannah!' her mother cried, 'I thought you were safe in
Palestine. Why did you come back to this terrible place?'

'Do not ask me,' Hannah replied. 'They have tortured me
for the secret – if I tell you they will torture you too.'

The guard took them back to their cells. Hannah was
placed in solitary confinement. Her mother was imprisoned in
another part of the building. They were not allowed to meet.

Hannah persuaded the guards to pass on messages, and when they were marchd outside for exercise, she would pretend to tie her shoelace while the others went past, and stand up again when she found herself next to her mother. A few words could be said before they were separated. In her cell, she put her bed under the small window high up in the wall. She put her table on the bed and her chair on the table. She climbed up and signalled through the window. Her mother, on the opposite side of the courtyard, could see her arms waving.

Then Hannah cut out letters of the alphabet and held them up to the window. In this way, she could talk to her mother and all the other prisoners in the cells opposite, giving them news and telling funny stories to cheer them up.

'Would you like to learn Hebrew?' she asked her mother.
'Yes,' came the reply.

Hannah cut out the letters of the Hebrew alphabet and
through the window she taught her mother the language she
had learned in Palestine.

One day, a guard brought a parcel to her mother. She
opened it, and inside she found a beautiful doll made of rags
and paper – the few things Hannah was allowed to have.
Soon Hannah was making dolls for everyone – especially for
the many children who had been imprisoned with their
mothers. Everyone loved Hannah.

The guards broke the rules and allowed her to see her
mother a few times. She entertained the children, singing
them songs and teaching them to read and write. She also
taught the adults – many of whom had never been to school.

Hannah continued to signal from her window. She told about a plot to kill Hitler, about the British victories, and how the war would soon be over. Everyone was happy. The Germans would leave and they would be free.

But the Nazi's did not give up easily. As they retreated they killed all the Jews they could in the prisons and concentration camps. One morning, Hannah was taken outside and shot. Only a few weeks later the war ended and the other prisoners were freed.

Everyone agreed that Hannah had made their life in prison bearable. She was the bravest person they had ever known.

Today in Israel there are thirty-two streets, a boat and two farms named after her.

HELM

Helm is a very special town. The people there are famous for being stupid, though they think they are very wise. They are also very honest, and they never go back on their word.

Shloime and his wife Gittel went to bed one night, and left the front door open.

'You must go and close the door,' Shloime said.

'No, you must go and close it,' said Gittel to Shloime.

'I cannot do that' said Shloime. 'I said you must close it, and I never go back on my word.'

'But I never go back on my word either,' said Gittel.

They agreed that the first person to speak should close the door. They lay in silence. The wind howled through the house. Icicles formed on the bedstead; snowflakes settled on the blankets. Neither spoke.

A band of robbers entered the house. They took all the copper saucepans and the silver candlesticks. Gittel said not a word. They took all the books and the clock. Shloime sat still.

'I am hungry,' one of the robbers said, 'Let's have a bite to eat.' They lit a fire and ate as much food as they could. Then they took the table, and the chairs; the stove and the carpets. They took the bookcases and the curtains; the wallpaper and the window-frames. Shloime and Gittel remained silent.

The thieves left, their hands so full of loot, they could not close the door.

The next morning, Gittel went out early to find food. Shloime sat on the floor. A travelling barber saw the door open and walked in.

'Do you need a hair cut?' he asked.

Shloime said nothing so the barber cut his hair.

'Well, how do you like it?' he said when he had finished. Shloime did not answer, so the barber cut off some more.

'You know, it might be better to shave it off completely,' the barber said. Shloime did not want his head shaved, but he was not going to speak. The barber shaved his head.

'Now,' said the barber, 'you owe me ten kopeks.'

Shloime had no money. He said nothing.

'What! You won't pay me?' shouted the barber. He went to the fireplace, gathered some soot and smeared it all over Shloime's face. Still, Shloime did not utter a sound. The barber stormed out of the house, leaving the door open.

Some time later, Gittel returned. She saw her husband sitting on the floor, with a bald head and sooty face, and screamed.

'My poor Shloime! What have they done to you?'

Shloime stood up, triumphant. 'You spoke first!' he said. 'Now go and close the door.'

BACKGROUND NOTES

THE LIE AND EVIL ENTER THE ARK

In Jewish tradition, countless stories based on the Bible have developed over the centuries. Such tales were used for teaching purposes and are part of a collection known as Midrash. This tale is a Midrash. It seeks to explain why, despite the destruction wrought by the flood, the world remained as corrupt as it had been before.

HOW JUDAH SAVED THE JEWS

The Jewish revolt against Syria led by Judah in 168 BCE is celebrated during an eight day festival called Hanukah. The events described in the story are based on the First Book of Maccabees in the Apocrypha, though the miracle with the oil is a later story.

This was one of many incidents when Jewish worship has been prohibited, and during the persecution, Judaism gained many martyrs. The quotation from Zechariah 4: 6; 'Not by my might,... but by My Spirit' became a message of hope to Jews in times of persecution, and is a comment on the fact of Jewish survival despite the extraordinary odds against it.

THE OVERCROWDED HOUSE

Poverty has been a feature of Jewish life throughout the ages. In most societies, Jews were second-class citizens, often forbidden to own land or practise certain trades. This was usually accepted with a quiet resignation. Jews developed a wry sense of humour which helped ease the situation a little and they were very good at laughing at themselves. This story is typical of East European humour.

HANNAH SENESH

Two events are important for the understanding of modern Jewry: the holocaust and the establishment of the state of Israel. This story, a biography rather than a legend, has been included as it touches on both. Hannah Senesh is a national folk hero in Israel where she has captured the imagination of young people for two generations. Her poetry is well known, and some poems set to music have been popular hits.

HELM

Every culture has its 'idiots'; in Jewish Eastern Europe they lived in Helm, a small town in Poland. The people of Helm are not really stupid, they follow a stubborn logic of their own, regardless of what experience and the world teaches. Hence they conclude that a spoon stirred in tea sweetens it, and sugar is only added to tell you how long to keep stirring.
Helm stories are satirical. We laugh at Shloime and Gittel, their stubbornness, and lack of any sense of proportion, but really we behave no differently.

A NOTE ABOUT DATES

Because of the Christian nature of the terms BC and AD, Jews usually refer to dates as BCE or CE: that is, Before the Common Era and Common Era.